STARDUST
SCHOOL OF
D☆NCE

BERTIE the Ninja Dancer

FOR PIP & FREYA - ZL

FIVE MILE

Five Mile
the publishing division of Regency Media
www.fivemile.com.au

First published 2019

NATIONAL LIBRARY OF AUSTRALIA

A catalogue record for this
book is available from the
National Library of Australia

ISBN: 9781760684617 (paperback)
Printed in Australia by Ovato 5 4 3 2

STARDUST
SCHOOL OF
D☆NCE

BERTIE the Ninja Dancer

BY ZANNI LOUISE
ART BY SR. SÁNCHEZ

FIVE MILE

CHAPTER ONE

Bertie was hanging upside-down like a bat in the willow tree.

She swung herself slowly back and forth, and listened to the sounds on the other side of the tall stone wall.

Just over the wall, cars whooshed by. She could hear the soft mutter of girls talking as they walked along Blossom Lane.

Hanging upside-down like this, Bertie decided that the willow tree was the best thing about her new fake home.

With its long, green ribbons of leaves to hide among and squiggly branches for climbing, the tree was the perfect hideout for a ninja like Bertie.

She swung herself upright and sat balanced on the branch. She pulled her special pen out of her pocket. Its gold plastic sparkled in the dappled light.

The little ballerina on the end of the pen smiled at her. 'Hello, Tiny

Dancer,' said Bertie, smiling back.

The pen's gold plastic was all scratched and Tiny Dancer's shoe paint had worn away long ago. But Bertie still kept the pen. She had to.

Besides, if she squinted, she could see Tiny Dancer was actually a ninja warrior. Just like her.

Bertie pulled her secret ninja diary from her front pocket, and scribbled a new entry on a fresh page.

Ninja Bertie takes in her fake home from

the safety of her hideout. No Fake Brother

sightings so far. Dad is talking to Fake Mum

in the kitchen. Now they are kissing. Ew.

Ninja Bertie wishes she hadn't seen that.

Bertie slipped the diary and her pen deep into her front pocket. In one fast move, she hunched into a ball and somersaulted off the branch.

'And that, my friends, is another perfect landing by Bertie Black,' she announced to the empty backyard. 'Please put your hands together for our champion!'

Bertie was so busy listening for the pretend applause, she didn't hear footsteps moving across the lawn. She didn't see a pudgy hand, with its chipped nails, reach out for something gold lying in the grass.

Until it was too late.

It was Fake Brother Marcus. He held Bertie's pen close to his nose.

'Wow, you're a ballet girl, Bertie Black! I wouldn't have guessed that. Let me take this pen off your hands.'

'Give it back, Marcus,' Bertie hissed through clenched teeth. She leapt towards the pen in one graceful move.

But Marcus was too quick.

He held it out of her reach. 'Nice try, Bertie. But I'm keeping it.' He turned and trotted off, holding the pen high in the air.

Bertie scampered silently up the willow's trunk.

As Marcus passed by below, she pinched the pen from his grip. With the pen between her teeth, she scaled up the tree, leaping from one branch to another with ease. Almost to the top.

'Hey! Come back here!' yelled Marcus.

'Nice try, Marcus. But I'm pretty sure I'm keeping my pen,' she shouted, feeling like a champion.

Bertie watched Marcus hover at the bottom of the tree.

Is Marcus waiting for me to give in?

she wondered to herself. *Never!*

Marcus did not know that Bertie was a tree ninja. She would never give in. And she would never ever, not in a million years, give Marcus her pen.

'I'm telling Mum you're not sharing,' Marcus called up the tree before heading back inside the house.

Bertie dropped down a few branches to look into the kitchen window. Bertie saw Marcus waving his arms about. Dianne, her fake mum, started waving her arms around too.

Bertie guessed they were saying mean things about what a terrible sharer she was.

Bertie slumped on the branch. She wasn't sure that she cared what her new step family said about her. She knew she wasn't a terrible sharer. That pen was important to her.

Bertie's real mum gave her that pen the night ballerinas danced *Peter and the Wolf* at a Ballet in the Park performance. The night of fairy lights and hot chips. The night of lemon sorbet and Mum cuddles. The best night of Bertie's life.

That pen was everything.

Bertie closed her eyes. It was like she was there. She could see the fairy lights, the dancers and Mum. She could even hear the ballet music.

Wait. She *could* hear the ballet music! Bertie's eyes snapped open. *Is my memory coming alive? Where is that music coming from?* She had to know.

Bertie checked for Marcus and then swung down the tree trunk.

She used the branch hanging over the tall stone wall to lower herself onto the other side.

With a short drop Bertie was on Blossom Lane.

On the other side of the road, the yellow door of a small wooden hall hung open. Ah, that was where the music was coming from.

Bertie carefully crossed the road and followed the music into the hall. Inside, its mirrored walls made the small space seem bigger than it was.

The main room was empty. Except for the

sound of music. It was coming out of an old blue stereo that sat on the wooden floor.

Bertie had not heard that piece of music since she was four. But she knew for certain what it was.

Without thinking, Bertie hugged her arms around herself and swayed.

Her left foot inched out to the left. Her right foot pointed and swung forward. One arm soared outwards. The other rose above her head.

Bertie spun like a cotton reel through the warm hall, unravelling to the music.

With her eyes now closed and the music carrying her, Bertie truly felt like she was there. There with her mother, watching the ballerinas perform *Peter and the Wolf* in the park. No. It was better than that.

In that moment, Bertie *was* one of those dancers.

A soft voice broke the spell. 'Ah, you are a natural.'

Bertie opened her eyes. Her feet stilled. Her arms lowered. A lady with dark hair was staring at Bertie, gentling clapping and with a broad smile across her face.

'Bravo,' said the lady, still clapping. 'Please don't let me stop you. That was magnificent.'

Bertie's cheeks burned like fierce embers.

CHAPTER TWO

'Sorry. I was just leaving.' Bertie ran out the yellow door.

She was standing on Blossom Lane, ready to cross, when a voice called behind her. 'Wait!'

Bertie turned. The lady stood at the hall's yellow door, her shawl wrapped around her. 'I was about to make cocoa. Do you like cocoa?'

Bertie definitely did.

'Yes, please,' she heard herself say. 'I'd love a cocoa.'

'Come in then,' said the lady.

Bertie was soon standing in the doorway of the tiny kitchen behind the dance studio. She watched as the lady shuffled around, finding cups and heating milk.

The music from *Peter and the Wolf* was still playing. Bertie's memories of that night in the park were still dancing around in her head. But she tried not to think about it.

Bertie looked around at the paintings of ballerinas that hung on the kitchen walls.

Past the paintings, she could see herself in the mirrored walls of the hall. *Ninja Bertie, waiting for cocoa in a ballet hall*, she thought. *What am I still doing here?*

'Here you go,' said the lady.

Steam dancers rose from Bertie's mug of cocoa.

When Bertie cradled the chipped red mug, the warmth trickled from her palms, up her arms and through her belly. When she sipped, the warmth spread to her toes.

'Thank you,' she murmured.

The lady was watching her, her big red lips smiling. 'You're welcome. Cocoa warms the soul, wouldn't you say?'

How did the lady know?

'I'm Madam Martine,' the lady continued, as Bertie sipped. 'And this is Stardust School of Dance – my very own dance academy.'

Bertie looked all around her.

'Academy' was a very fancy word. The hall didn't look very fancy. It looked like it needed to be painted. And maybe a new bulb to replace the one that flickered in the corner lamp. But she didn't say that.

'I'm Bertie,' she said.

Madam Martine kept smiling at her.

Bertie felt uncomfortable, like she should say more. 'I like that music,' she said finally, pointing to the stereo. 'It's *Peter and the Wolf*, isn't it?'

Madam Martine's face exploded into a wide smile. She clapped her hands. 'Yes! Yes! How did you know? Most of my students wouldn't know the name of that ballet!' She nodded slowly. 'I could tell you are a dancer, Bertie.'

Bertie shook her head and looked at the floor. She wasn't a dancer. She was a ninja. But she didn't say anything.

'Bertie, I have something very important to ask you,' said Madam Martine.

Uh-oh. Bertie really didn't like important questions.

'Would you perhaps be our Peter?' asked Madam Martine.

Huh? But Bertie stayed quiet.

'Our Peter,' Madam Martine said. 'If one of my older classes were to do a *Peter and the Wolf* performance, we'd need a Peter. You'd be perfect.'

Bertie gasped. No-one had ever said she was perfect before. Not at anything. Especially not at Peter!

'No, I am sorry, Madam Martine, but I can't. Really, I can't dance.'

A clatter of shoes on the floorboards made Bertie spin around. A crowd of little kids were rushing into the hall.

Some wore tutus. Some wore leotards. Some were barefooted.

Others wore dance shoes.

'Ah, it's my Tiny Tots class!' said
Madam Martine.

Bertie hadn't seen this many kids
since finishing up at her old school
two weeks ago. That was when her
dad made her move to Blossom
Lane. She slid her unfinished mug
of cocoa onto the nearest bench.
Then she unfolded into an invisible
ninja leap, making her escape
before anyone tried to talk to her.
She landed on the footpath outside.

'Bertie? Please, think about it?'
called Madam Martine after her.

Bertie didn't need to think about it.

She couldn't be Peter. Bertie Black didn't perform. Performances were for people with two real parents, who bought them flowers and hugged them after the show. Bertie didn't have those things.

She crossed the road safely. In one leap, she pulled herself onto the branch of the willow tree and back over the stone wall.

Just because Bertie couldn't perform, it didn't stop her huddling in the shadow of the willow leaves, watching the tiny hall that smelt of sunshine and cocoa.

CHAPTER THREE

Sluuuuurp!

Marcus grinned, and looked up at Bertie. A long strand of spaghetti hung between his front teeth. Tomato sauce made a ring around his mouth.

Sluuurp!

'Ew,' said Bertie, frowning.

Marcus checked to make sure his mum was still in the kitchen.

Then he turned back to Bertie.
He let the spaghetti slide from his
mouth, back into his bowl.

'I can't watch,' said Bertie,
pushing back her chair to leave
the table.

'Bertie, in this house we stay
seated until we are finished eating,'
said Fake Mum, putting garlic
bread on the table. 'Here. Have
some bread.'

'No, thanks,' muttered Bertie.
'I've lost my appetite.'

'If you aren't eating, then wait
until your brother has finished,
please,' said Bertie's dad, coming

into the room and sitting down.

Bertie squirmed. *Brother? No thanks*, she thought. Marcus was not her brother. But she pulled back her chair and sat down again. She always listened to her dad.

Marcus grinned at Bertie and slurped again. Bits of sauce flicked in her direction. Three red blobs landed on the front pocket of her jeans. She wiped them furiously. She was so busy getting rid of Marcus's mess, it took her a moment to realise her pocket was flat.

Empty.

Penless.

Bertie's chair scraped as she stood.

'Bertie!' said her dad, sounding serious. 'Dianne asked you to sit down while we eat, please!'

'I can't, Dad. I've lost something. Something important.'

Bertie flew out the back door and leapt across the garden. There was just enough evening light to search by. She patted the grass under the willow. She scampered up into its branches and hopped from branch to branch. She felt around in tree forks, and in clusters of leaves.

No pen.

'Bertie! Come down!' Fake Mum called up the tree.

Bertie could see Fake Mum standing at the base of the willow tree.

She watched as Fake Mum turned her face up to the tree and spoke softly.

'Bertie, I know it can't be easy for you coming here so suddenly. But I'll do anything to make this work. Bertie? Are you safe up there? Come down. Let's talk.'

Fake Mum's voice sounded kind. But Bertie felt certain that Fake Mum couldn't really understand.

Bertie stayed silent. She waited for Fake Mum to go inside, then whizzed down the tree trunk to the ground. *Where is my pen?*

Her first thought was Marcus. Marcus stole her pen. But how? He couldn't reach into her front pocket. There's no way a ninja would miss an obvious move like that.

No. Bertie had to clear her head.

I need to think calmly. Now, where have I been?

Then Bertie saw herself, twirling like a fool in front of mirrored walls. *Of course. Stardust School of Dance.*

Bertie must have lost her pen when she was dancing!

She was meant to be inside at the dinner table. But this was important. Bertie clambered back into the tree, over the wall and dropped, like a ninja, onto Blossom Lane.

The light was still on in the hall. Music echoed out. She checked for cars and crossed.

From the doorway, Bertie watched a small group of dancers holding hands, in a circle. It wasn't the Tiny Tots group. These dancers were older, Bertie's age.

The circle was spinning, while princess music played. The dancers bounced up and down. It was like a circle of popping corn.

There was one girl with long blonde hair who looked excited as she sprung up and down. Her back was very straight. A boy in a coat and top hat kept jumping out of the circle, clicking his heels and then

rejoining the others.

'Well done, my Bright Sparks!' called Madam Martine. 'Dance your hearts out!'

Bertie thought it was generous of Madam Martine to call this popping around 'dancing'. It was definitely no *Peter and the Wolf*.

CHAPTER FOUR

Madam Martine switched off the music and clapped her hands. 'Thank you for all your hard work this evening! In our next class, let's talk about our performance.'

One girl, with very dark hair, bent to untie her shoe ribbons. As she did, a tiny sausage dog appeared from under the seat and ran towards her. The girl laughed.

From the doorway of the hall, Bertie laughed too.

'Petit Jeté! There you are!' the girl said as the little dog licked her face.

Bertie watched the boy in the hat swing a cane from side to side. The blonde girl was twirling now, as if lost in a dream.

'Bertie, you came back!' said Madam Martine, standing in the doorway. 'You've changed your mind, I see!'

'Actually, Madam M, I'm here about my pen. I must have dropped it here. When I was, well, you know ... ' Bertie stepped out of the hall light.

'Ah! Your pen!' said Madam Martine. 'What does it look like, Bertie?'

'It's gold. Sparkly. With a dancer on the end. She could be a ninja. Anyway. It's gold.'

'Here,' said the boy, pulling a pen from his jacket pocket. 'I carry this around with me. Just in case anyone needs my autograph. But you can have it. I'll get another one.'

Bertie looked at the plain blue pen in the boy's hand. 'It's okay, thanks. You keep it.'

'I'm Edmund,' said the boy, tucking the pen back in his pocket.

'I'm Bertie,' said Bertie.

'Are you a dancer too?' asked Edmund. 'You could join our class. We're the Bright Sparks.'

'Um, thanks,' said Bertie. 'But I'm not a dancer.' She didn't tell Edmund she was a ninja, because ninjas kept their identity a secret.

'I'm Priya,' said the dark-haired girl, still giggling as the dog licked her chin. 'And that's Lulu Lullaby.' She pointed at the light-haired girl spinning.

Lulu waved, then spun away from them, her hair flattening into a white curtain behind her.

'Petit Jeté and I will help you find your pen,' Priya said, smiling widely at Bertie. 'Won't we, Petit Jeté?'

Priya put Petit Jeté on the ground

before Bertie could say anything. The sausage dog nuzzled everyone's legs. Bertie couldn't help grinning and she bent down to tickle the little dog's fur. She didn't think Petit Jeté would be much help. But he sure was cute.

Priya got down on her hands and knees and looked under chairs. Edmund looked in the little kitchen. Madam Martine checked her drawers. While Lulu danced in circles, Bertie pulled open the red velvet curtains, which hung at the back of the hall. Behind the curtains was a small stage. But no pen.

'Looks like it's not here after all,' said Bertie. 'But thanks for your help.' Bertie waved as she headed out of the hall.

'Bye, Bertie!' called Edmund and Priya.

'Byyyye!' sang Lulu, as she danced.

Madam Martine was hobbling after Bertie. As she approached, she winced, and held her hip.

'Are you okay, Madam M?' asked Bertie.

'Oh, yes. This is a very old injury.'

'What happened?' asked Bertie.

'It was the night of my first

performance as prima ballerina for the New York Ballet, actually,' said Madam Martine. Her smile was small, like she remembered something sad. 'I was running for a bus, when I collided with a bicycle. It wasn't anyone's fault. Still. I miss dancing.'

'You don't dance?'

'No, Bertie. Not with my body. But my heart and my mind will never stop dancing. And now I get to teach. That is as good as dancing. Watching young blossoms bloom. Blossoms like yourself, Bertie.'

'Um, I'm not a blossom, Madam M.'

Madam Martine's red smile widened. 'But maybe you're a Peter,' she said. 'Any chance you've changed your mind? You know, it's not too late for us to do *Peter and the Wolf*.'

'Err ... I'm a bit busy, Madam M,' said Bertie quickly. 'I have a pen to find.' Bertie hoped she didn't sound rude.

But Madam Martine didn't seem upset.

'Can you guess what part I was performing, Bertie? The night of my accident? My first and last night as prima ballerina for the New York Ballet?'

Bertie had no clue.

'Peter, from *Peter and the Wolf*. My favourite ballet.' Madam Martine smiled gently. 'Goodnight, Bertie.'

Bertie waved as she crossed the road. On the other side, she pulled herself up the stone wall, over, and dropped back into the garden.

Maybe the willow tree wasn't the only good thing about her new home.

CHAPTER FIVE

A week later, Bertie used her dad's black pen to scribble down recent events in her ninja diary.

> Marcus keeps asking Ninja Bertie to play
> Monopoly. Ninjas don't play Monopoly.
>
> Fake Mum wants to take Ninja Bertie to
> a yoga class. Um, yoga? Ninja Bertie is not into
> yoga.

> Dad is giving Ninja Bertie way too many
>
> bear hugs.
>
> Ninja Bertie can't stop thinking about
>
> those nice kids at the dance school. Can
>
> ninjas and dancers be friends? Uncertain.
>
> Ninja Bertie is still on the lookout for
>
> Tiny Dancer pen. Must stay focussed!

Knock, knock.

'Hey, Bertie! Wanna play Chasey?' Marcus called through the door.

'No, thanks, Marcus,' she called back.

There was silence.

Knock, knock. Knock, knock. Knock, knock. Knock, knock. Knock, knock. Knock, knock.

Bertie threw open the door. 'Marcus!' she sighed. 'I'm trying to concentrate!'

She pushed past Marcus and ran out to the willow. Stuffing her diary into her jeans pocket, she climbed as high as she could. One thing was for sure, Marcus would not climb after her.

He stood under the tree for a while, calling up about Chasey, and UNO and marbles. Bertie was

not in the mood. She watched him
move slowly around the garden.
After a few minutes, he trudged
back inside.

From her high-up view, Bertie
could see over the backyard's tall
stone wall. She could see cars
passing, and the roof of the little
hall. Then she spotted the girl from
last week. Priya, the one with the
dog. She was with her dad, walking
down Bertie's side of Blossom Lane.

Bertie squinted. Her keen ninja
vision helped her to see that
Priya was holding something. But
it was too small to be Petit Jeté.

It was definitely alive, though. And squirmy!

The yellow thing plopped out of Priya's hands, and onto the street. It scurried towards the road!

'Stop, Quacky!' called Priya, running after it.

'Careful, Priya! You must not run onto the road!' said her dad, pulling Priya back.

Bertie swung down from the tree in a single move and reached for the duckling, just as it stepped off the gutter. A blue truck zoomed by. Bertie pulled back.

Bertie crouched for a moment,

stroking the duckling's soft back, and staring into its startled eyes.

'Bertie! Were you in the tree?' asked Priya. 'You saved Quacky!'

'I couldn't let him cross the road alone,' said Bertie. The duckling nuzzled her cheek, as if to say thank you. Bertie chuckled.

'Priya, you'll be late for dance class,' her dad said. 'And I don't know what to do with that duck while you are dancing. I told you to leave it at home.'

'Do you want to come to class too, Bertie?' asked Priya. 'You can hold Quacky. If you want.'

Bertie was about to tell Priya she was too busy. But then Quacky nibbled her finger.

'Okay, I'll come,' said Bertie. 'I'll keep Quacky safe while you dance.'

And I'll keep an eye out for my pen, she thought to herself.

'Thank you, Bertie!' said Priya, and tugged Bertie's free hand to pull her towards the hall.

Bertie held Quacky to her chest, as she watched the dancers leap around to warm up.

They scurried into a circle around Madam Martine.

'Right, my magnificent dancers!'

said Madam Martine. 'What are we going to do for our performance?'

'*Cinderella*!' called Lulu.

'*Singin' in the Rain*!' said Edmund.

'*Swan Lake*!' sang Priya.

Madam Martine glanced at Bertie. 'Any ideas, Bertie?'

'What about doing *Peter and the Wolf*?' said Bertie, knowing that Madam Martine had been thinking about it.

'You know, Priya,' Bertie said, 'you could be the little bird. And Quacky could be the duck! He's already got the costume.'

'I vote *Peter and the Wolf*!' said

Priya, with a laugh.

'Edmund, you would make a good wolf. You could wear a tuxedo!' said Bertie.

'Can the wolf really wear a tuxedo?' asked Edmund.

'He wore one in the version I saw,' said Bertie.

'Ladies and gentlemen,' said Edmund, standing, his cane raised. 'I also vote *Peter and the Wolf*. As you were.'

'Lulu, you could be the cat. The cat is graceful. Like you,' said Bertie.

Lulu grinned. '*Peter and the Wolf*!' she cheered.

51

Madam Martine clasped her hands together. 'Wonderful! Just one thing. Who will be our Peter?'

She looked over at Bertie again. Bertie said nothing.

'Bertie's not a dancer,' said Edmund.

'I saw Bertie do some very cool moves outside,' said Priya. 'She rescued Quacky, actually. I reckon Bertie really can dance.'

'My grandma says a true dancer doesn't always wear a tutu,' said Lulu, her eyes widening. 'I guess Grandma is talking about dancers like Bertie. Maybe Bertie is a dancer in disguise!'

Bertie felt her cheeks redden. She didn't think she was a dancer in disguise.

But now she thought about it, Peter was basically a dancing ninja shepherd! *Maybe I can manage that. How hard can it be?* Then she had another thought. Coming to the dance hall every week for rehearsals would give her a chance to find that pen.

'Okay. I'll be Peter,' said Bertie, finally.

The hall filled with the sound of clapping and hooting.

Bertie grinned around at her new friends and Madam Martine, whose smile was the widest Bertie had ever seen it.

When the cheering stopped, Bertie spoke again. 'But, Priya, can I ask you something?'

'Sure!' said Priya.

'Do you mind if I hold Quacky during the performance?' Quacky nuzzled Bertie's neck. 'The duck is one of Peter's best friends, you know.'

'Of course you can!' said Priya. 'Quacky clearly loves you!'

'That's decided then,' said

Madam Martine. 'This season, Stardust School of Dance's Bright Sparks class will perform *Peter and the Wolf*!'

Madam Martine's skirt billowed behind her as she hobbled around to switch on the music.

CHAPTER SIX

The week before the next dance class, Bertie's secret ninja diary looked like this.

Ninja Bertie accidentally signs up for dance.

Whoops!

Ninja Bertie will definitely chicken out.

> Ninjas do not chicken out of things, Bertie.
>
> True. Ninja Bertie will go to ballet.

> Ninja Bertie will not go to ballet.

> Ninja Bertie will go to ballet. Be brave,
>
> Ninja Bertie!

Five minutes before class, Bertie pulled on her black lycra ninja pants, which were the closest thing she could find to a dance costume. She used the willow tree to swing onto the stone wall. Perched on the wall, she looked across at the hall.

Bertie felt sure she had swallowed a beehive. Her belly was buzzing.

'Breathe, Bertie Black,' she whispered to herself. 'You'll be fine.'

She pounced off the wall onto Blossom Lane, checked for cars and scooted across the road into the hall.

'Bertie! Here's Quacky.' Priya ran towards her. She dropped the yellow duckling in Bertie's hands.

'Um, thanks,' said Bertie, holding Quacky.

Quacky nibbled Bertie's chin. She laughed. The bees in her tummy calmed down.

'Dancers, your attention, please!' said Madam Martine. 'In the first dance, we meet each of the characters. Priya, the bird, you're up first.'

Madam Martine turned on the old stereo. A flute played.

Bertie remembered the song clearly from the night of Ballet in the Park. The memory sent a lightning bolt through Bertie's belly as she watched Priya move gracefully across the hall.

'Priya, I want you to improvise,' said Madam Martine. 'How do you feel a bird should move?'

Priya put her hands on her hips and turned her feet outward.

She bent her knees, then sprang like a little bird fluttering through the garden.

'Now, Quacky, this one's for you,' said Madam Martine. 'I don't need to tell you how to be a duck.'

An oboe played. Bertie placed Quacky on the floor. He waddled in a small circle, then raced back to Bertie.

'Well done, Quacky!' said Madam Martine.

'And now for the cat! Lulu, please show us your inner cat!' said Madam Martine.

A clarinet played. Lulu crawled

and arched her back. She licked the back of her hand, then stalked around the hall on tip-toes. Lulu was so busy becoming her inner cat, she didn't see Madam Martine's orange chair. Lulu landed with a thud.

'Are you okay?' asked Bertie, racing over with Quacky. She held her spare hand out to Lulu. Lulu let Bertie help her up.

'I'm fine. I'm used to falling,' said Lulu. She leapt away, like a cat pouncing off a wall. She tucked herself into a ball and purred.

'Edmund,' said Madam Martine.

'I simply must see your wolf! Er ...
Edmund?'

Bertie, Priya, Lulu and Madam
Martine turned to each other.
Where was Edmund?

'Edmund?' Madam Martine
called again.

They heard *tap-tap-tap* from
the changeroom. The tapping got
louder and louder. It sounded like
rain on a metal roof.

In swirled Edmund, in a bowtie
and tuxedo, his arms outstretched,
his feet moving like wheels on a
train. Faster, faster, faster! He did
the polka, a lively hop-step dance,

across the hall and howled, and tapped and howled again.

Everyone laughed and clapped. Only Quacky buried himself into the crook of Bertie's elbow, desperate to get away from the dancing wolf.

'Oh my!' said Madam Martine, still laughing. 'Edmund, that was the most elegant wolf I have ever seen! How I love your tuxedo!

'Now, for our Peter. The one who brings it all together. Bertie, close your eyes, feel the music, and dance!'

Bertie's eyes were not closed.

They were wide open, staring at
Madam Martine, then Priya, then
Lulu, then Edmund. She focussed
on Quacky's tiny yellow head.

Bertie didn't move, but her
mind was racing. She had made a
mistake. She shouldn't have come.
She should have stayed in her tree,
on her own, like a ninja, working
out how to find her pen. The bees
raged in her tummy.

Madam Martine pressed play on
the blue stereo. Peter's happy song
rippled through the hall.

Bertie was sucked back into the
memory of Peter prancing around

the park. Without warning, the dance rose inside her, like steam on hot cocoa.

With Quacky tucked tight to her chest, Bertie leapt across the dance hall. She sprung onto a chair and landed on one foot. She hopped from one end of the hall to the other, as if picking her way through long grass.

Bertie twirled towards Priya. 'Hold Quacky,' she whispered.

Bertie ran across the hall and, when she had enough momentum, flipped through the air. She landed in a neat crouch.

She stood and raised
her arms.

*Another perfect landing
by Bertie Black*, she said to
herself.

This time, she didn't have
to imagine it. A real crowd
was applauding.

Warmth trickled to
Bertie's toes, filling every
part of her.

CHAPTER SEVEN

Bertie's fake mum spun around when Bertie entered the kitchen after class.

'Where have you been, Bertie? I have been worried sick! I was about to call your dad at work.'

Bertie was ninja silent. She couldn't lie. But she couldn't say she'd been at Stardust. Fake Mum might stop her going.

'Bertie?'

Bertie ran out of the kitchen, to her willow. She scrambled up into the branches.

'Bertie, please,' called Fake Mum from below. 'You need to tell me where you've been. You can't just disappear like that. We are family. I care about you.'

Bertie's heart beat loudly in her ears. *Family?*

She could hear Marcus whistling nearby. From behind the hanging willow leaves, Bertie saw him trundle towards them, his hands in his pockets.

'She's been dancing,' said Marcus, casually. 'Across the road. In the hall. I saw her.'

Bertie's cheeks flamed. *How dare Marcus spy on me?*

Bertie saw confusion spread across her fake mum's face. The confusion turned slowly into a smile.

'That's wonderful news!' said Fake Mum. 'When Marcus told me about your special ballet pen, I thought I could enrol you at Stardust School of Dance. I was planning to ask you tonight what you thought.'

Something was slowly uncurling in Bertie's chest. Dianne was very thoughtful for a fake mum.

Bertie whittled down the trunk and pulled a crumpled sheet of paper from her back pocket. She handed it to Dianne.

Dear Parents and Friends,
You are cordially invited to the gala performance of Peter and the Wolf.
5pm, Sunday 25 April.

Please RSVP to Madam Martine.

Bertie gave Dianne a chance to
read the invitation, then plucked
it from her hands. She stuffed
the invitation into her pocket and
clambered back into her tree.

'We'd absolutely love to come!'
called Dianne, smiling up at Bertie.
'I'll call Madam Martine right
away.'

Bertie smiled too.

CHAPTER EIGHT

It was performance night. Ninja Bertie had been learning some cool new moves at Stardust over the last few weeks. She had also been working on some new ninja dance moves of her own, including a high kick and flick, and spinning in the air like a tornado. These moves would also come in handy if Ninja Bertie ever had to save the world.

It was almost time for Ninja Bertie to go on stage. She was feeling as calm as a lake, thanks to practising the new breathing technique Dianne had taught her. Dianne called it yoga breathing. But Bertie thought it should be called ninja breathing.

With everything that had been going on, Ninja Bertie still hadn't found her Tiny Dancer pen. But tonight Ninja Bertie was focussed on giving the best performance she could.

Even Bertie had to admit that the hall looked pretty fancy.

She and the other kids had spent
all last weekend and every night
that week painting cardboard
props. Fairy lights were strung from
every corner of the hall and across
the little stage. That had been
Bertie's idea.

Madam Martine's dance hall was
filled with chatter and laughter.
Families, friends and even some
dancers from the other Stardust
classes had come along.

'Welcome, students, families
and friends of Stardust School
of Dance to *Peter and the Wolf*!'
said Madam Martine, stepping in

front of the closed velvet curtains. The hall stilled. 'The dancers from our Bright Sparks class have worked very hard to bring you this performance. So please, sit back, and absorb the wonder that is *Peter and the Wolf*!'

The hall darkened. The fairy lights twinkled.

Madam Martine stood at the edge of the stage. 'I'm going to tell you the story of *Peter and the Wolf*,' she said. 'If you listen carefully you will hear that every character is represented by a different instrument in the orchestra.'

Wearing too much make-up and crazy costumes, Bertie and the others huddled behind the curtains offstage. Petit Jeté wound around Bertie's ankles. Even the little dog couldn't bear to miss the fun.

A few bees buzzed in Bertie's belly. But on the whole, it was pretty quiet in there.

The flute played. 'Good luck!'

whispered Bertie, as Priya flitted onto the stage.

The oboe played. Quacky waddled out. The audience cheered and laughed.

Lulu slunk on stage when the clarinet played.

Edmund tapped his feet furiously to the sound of the horns.

Backstage, Bertie pressed her nails into her palms. 'Breathe, Bertie Black,' she whispered in the darkness. She was on next.

And that's when she saw it. A stroke of glittered gold plastic, peeking out of Priya's backpack.

Bertie's special pen glinted in the stage light. She hadn't lost it. Priya had stolen her pen! The bees went mad. Bertie thought Priya was a friend. A real friend. But Priya was a pen thief!

Bertie swiped the pen, tucking it deep into the pocket of her silly Peter pants. She became a tight ball and, silent as a ninja, scurried from behind the curtains, out the door and into the cool night.

Peter's string solo rang through the hall.

CHAPTER NINE

In her tree, tucked behind a curtain of leaves, Bertie shivered. She wiped something wet from her cheek.

Yuck. Tears. Bertie hated tears. Ninjas shouldn't cry. That was ninja rule 517, or something.

The worst bit was that Bertie had been starting to like her new home. Dianne was actually nice.

The willow tree was awesome. And she could put up with Fake Brother Marcus because there was a dance hall across the road. She had a dance teacher who believed in her. And friends ...

Or so she had thought.

The strains of music travelled across the street to the branch where Bertie sat.

Peter's tune played for a bit, then cut out. Bertie could hear Madam Martine's microphone voice, but couldn't hear the words. She waited for the music to come back on. Instead, she heard voices. The hall door opened. The dark shapes of parents, brothers, sisters, grandparents and a string of dancers spilled onto the street.

'Bertie!'

'Bertie!'

'Bertie, where are you?' they called.

Bertie tucked herself tighter and pulled her leaf curtain closed.

'Maybe she went home,' said a voice. Bertie couldn't tell who.

'I think I know,' said another. Bertie recognised that voice. Priya.

Bertie shrunk. She hushed her breath.

Through the leaves, Bertie watched Priya, who was dressed as a colourful bird, wait for a van to pass, then cross the road. She carried Quacky in her arms and her backpack on her shoulder. Petit Jeté clipped her heels.

'Bertie? Are you up there?' Priya called up the tree. 'In case you are, I've got a present for you. Maybe it'll help your nerves.'

Priya rifled through her bag.
'Well, I thought I had a present
for you. It was in here ... Stay, Petit
Jeté! You're making it hard for me to
look.'

Bertie wondered what present
Priya could have for her. *Why would
Priya steal from Bertie, then get her a
present?*

Bertie edged forward on the
branch. But she stayed hidden.

'Don't get too excited,' said Priya.
'It's just a pen.'

Bertie's breath stuck.

'A ballet pen,' continued Priya.

'Like the one you lost. A girl at school had one. I swapped it for Lucy, one of my guinea-pig babies.'

What? Bertie thought. She slowly shuffled along the branch. The leaves shuddered, giving away her position.

Priya moved closer to the branch. Bertie could see Priya squinting up, through the hanging leaves.

'I'm sorry, Bertie. But the pen has disappeared,' Priya said. 'I have no idea where it went.'

'I do,' said Bertie. She scaled down the tree to the wall. She held out the pen for Priya to see.

'You have it?' said Priya. 'I don't understand.'

'I ... stole it,' said Bertie, her voice as big as a sesame seed. 'I just thought ...'

Bertie's dad and Dianne ran across the street, followed by Madam Martine.

'There you are, Bertie!' cried her dad. 'Thank goodness you're okay!'

'You must be very nervous, going on stage, Bertie. I would be!' said Dianne.

'I'm not nervous,' said Bertie, swinging off the wall onto the footpath. 'I was mad. But now I'm not. Now I realise what good friends I have. And how lucky I really am.'

She hugged Priya.

'Quack!' said Quacky, between them. Petit Jeté jumped up to join in the hug. Bertie's dad and Dianne also pulled Bertie close.

'Just one thing,' said Bertie. 'I'm not sure what we are still

doing outside. We have a dance to
perform!'

In the lamp light, Bertie could see
Madam Martine's red lips stretched
wide. Madam Martine led the
dancers and the audience, back
into the hall.

CHAPTER TEN

The little stage's curtains closed, then reopened. The audience cheered. Priya, Lulu and Edmund stood in a line. They bowed again.

'Come on, Bertie!' whispered Edmund.

Bertie skipped over to join them. She held Quacky under one arm.

The audience stood. The clapping and cheering thundered.

The dancers stretched out their hands to Madam Martine, who hobbled towards the stage. She carried a bunch of flowers, and handed one to each dancer.

'You are magnificent,' she whispered each time.

She handed Bertie a yellow rose.

'You are magnificent, Bertie,' said Madam Martine. 'And I am proud of you for coming back inside.'

Bertie's dad came up and gave her one of his famous bear hugs. Dianne came up to Bertie, too. She placed a giant bunch of daisies in her arms. She wrapped her arm around Bertie's shoulder.

'This was one of the nicest nights, Bertie,' Dianne said. 'I'd given up hope of Marcus getting into ballet.'

Bertie smiled. 'Thanks, Dianne,' she said. 'I'm glad you liked it.'

The bees in Bertie's tummy were sleepy. The hot cocoa feeling, though, spread through her, warming her up.

'Hey, Bertie, do you want to play hide-and-seek in the garden?' asked Edmund, unlacing his tap shoes. 'We are going to stick around for a bit, while the adults chat. You can be "it" if you like.'

Bertie started counting. Lulu, Edmund and Priya ran off. Priya cradled both animals.

'Bertie, isn't this yours? I found it under my chair.'

Bertie uncovered her eyes to look.

A gold sparkly pen lay in Marcus's pudgy palm.

There was a tiny dancer on the end, whose shoe paint had worn away.

Bertie held the pen to her chest. 'Thank you, Marcus! You probably think it's just a dumb pen. But you don't know what this means to me.'

Marcus shrugged. 'Glad I found it, then.'

'Do you want to play hide-and-seek too?' asked Bertie. 'You have to hide quickly though. I'm nearly up to twenty.'

Marcus hurried across the stage, dodging his way through the crowd.

'Seventeen, eighteen, nineteen, twenty! Ready or not, here I come!'

called Bertie, and darted through the Stardust School of Dance hall to find all her friends.

THE END

More about the STARDUST dancers

MADAM MARTINE

Madam Martine has always loved dance. When she was younger, she practised hard for many years and eventually became prima ballerina for the New York Ballet. Sadly, an accident meant Madam Martine could no longer dance. But it was then that she discovered she could always dance in her heart. And that she also loved to teach kids to dance. So she created Stardust School of Dance! Madam Martine loves hot cocoa, swirly dance skirts, and helping her young dancers realise their dreams.

BERTIE BLACK

Psst. Don't tell anyone, but Bertie Black is secretly a ninja. She keeps a secret ninja diary, and spends her spare time practising her awesome ninja moves. She's an aerial-flip specialist. But Ninja Bertie has recently discovered she also loves to dance. Bertie lives with her step family on Blossom Lane, just across the road from the Stardust School of Dance. She loves climbing trees, animals, perfecting her ninja moves and her new friends. She is part of Stardust's Bright Sparks class, with Priya, Edmund and Lulu.

LULU LULLABY

Lulu Lullaby lives with her grandma on Blossom Lane. Her grandma was once a famous ballet dancer, and she's taught Lulu everything she knows about ballet. Lulu knows all the fancy French names for ballet steps. As well as dancing, Lulu loves to daydream. She's also a very caring friend and granddaughter. Lulu dreams of being a famous dancer one day, just like her grandma. She is part of Stardust's Bright Sparks class, with Edmund, Priya and Bertie.

EDMUND FONTAINE

Edmund Fontaine's dad would like Edmund to be a chef, just like him. But Edmund is more interested in dance. Edmund spends rainy Sundays watching his favourite movie, *Singin' in the Rain*, and can perform Gene Kelly's dance routine perfectly. The only time you'll catch Edmund out of his tuxedo and top hat, is when he's wearing his dance clothes. Edmund is a good friend, and an excellent tap dancer! He is part of Stardust's Bright Sparks class, with Lulu, Bertie and Priya.

PRIYA PATEL

Priya Patel is an animal whisperer. She helps animals who are in trouble or need a friend. She and her sister Shaan have lots of pets at home, but Priya's closest companion is Petit Jeté, her sausage dog. Priya's mum is a vet. When Priya isn't spending her free time at Stardust School of Dance practising her moves and hanging out with her friends, she's most likely at the vet clinic helping her mum. She is part of Stardust's Bright Sparks class, with Bertie, Edmund and Lulu.

LULU
the Ballerina Dreamer

Lulu Lullaby knocks over Grandma's precious ballet trophy and it smashes into a million pieces! Lulu is heartbroken. But she wants to make things right. If only Lulu can get the lead role in Stardust's new performance of Cinderella, she just might be able to win her own trophy and make Grandma proud. Will Lulu's dreams come true?